The New Adventures of
Peter Rabbit

By Jane Resnick

Illustrated by Doug Cushman

Contents

The Tale of Peter's Egg . . . . . *page 5*

The Tale of Peter's

Swimming Lesson . . . . *page 14*

Published by
Joshua Morris Publishing, Inc.
167 Old Post Road
Southport, CT 06490

Printed in Korea

The Tale of PETER'S EGG

IT was a beautiful summer day and Peter Rabbit was daydreaming. He was lying under the tall leaves of the Tiger lillies by Mr. McGregor's barnyard. Mrs. Rabbit's birthday was coming up, and she loved eggs. Peter had a special egg in mind, one all purple with blackberry juice and nestled in a little basket of green ferns. Henrietta Hen had even promised him an egg, if he could only get into the hen house.

Peter stuck his nose in the fence, and peeked into the barnyard. "Where there are hens there must be eggs, but I can't get my paws on one at all!"

AND then Peter had the strangest sensation! He felt a movement beneath him, and jumped up to see the ground just barely and very rapidly breaking up into a zigzag line of little mounds. Every few seconds, a mole popped to the surface, dove back down, and kept moving along like a train on a crooked track. Peter ran ahead to where he thought the mole would come up again, and so he did. "Whatever are you doing, Martin Mole?" he asked. The mole answered, "I'm just dig, dig, digging. Is that you, Peter Rabbit?" (Moles have very poor eyesight, you know.) "Yes, Martin," Peter answered, "and am I glad to see you!"

Martin's digging had given Peter an idea. "Martin," he asked, "Can you dig your way under Mr. McGregor's fence?" "Of course I can," the mole replied. Peter watched excitedly through the fence as Martin's little tunnel made a line right into the middle of the chicken yard. Martin stuck his head up for an instant next to the beak of a big red hen and then he quickly burrowed back to Peter.

"Oh, my!" Peter exclaimed. "If only I could fit into your tunnel." "I don't know," Martin said. "But wait a minute—if my whole family helps, we could dig together and make a tunnel you *could* squeeze into!"

SO the next day, Peter waited impatiently for Martin to return with his brother and sisters. Suddenly, all around him the forest floor began to pucker up—leaves twitched and grass tumbled. Moles move very quickly and they haven't much time for conversation, so Martin and his family passed Peter right by as they dug to the hen house.

Peter stood with his mouth open as the little mounds of earth popped up all over the barnyard, under the wall of the hen house and back out again. The mole family emerged laughing and panting. They were having such a digging good time that they just couldn't resist going in all directions.

MARTIN shouted, "It's all yours!" as they vanished into the trembling earth. Peter stuck his nose into the opening of the tunnel and sniffed. He was a rabbit, after all, and lived in a lovely burrow beneath the root of a tree, so he knew there was nothing to be afraid of. But still . . . the tunnel was awfully dark, and it seemed terribly small, and the newly dug sides, were oh, so soft. Taking a deep breath and half closing his eyes, Peter began crawling.

K NOWING that the tunnel was not very deep and that he could poke his head up through the top gave him some comfort, but he didn't want to be caught inside the fence of Mr. McGregor's barnyard! So he kept crawling and crawling. All at once he heard a roar of chickens and hens clucking and chattering, a truly awful noise. Peter was under the hen house! He could see the end of the tunnel!

HE scrambled to the opening and lifted his head, gasping for air. The first hen who caught sight of him clucked wildly. Then a chorus rose up louder and louder.

Fortunately Henrietta Hen spotted him and clucked even louder than all the rest. "Over here, Peter," she cried. Peter rushed to Henrietta with chickens flapping all around him, pecking at his great rabbit ears. "This is for your mother," she told Peter, giving him the egg proudly. "Thank you," Peter said, hastily turning to go; for being in the hen house frightened him dreadfully.

JUST then, the door flew open and Mr. McGregor's big booted foot appeared. All at once, Mr. McGregor spotted Peter and dashed toward him. Peter, shaking with fear, held his egg tightly, kept his eye on the tunnel hole, and raced between Mr. McGregor's enormous feet. Running as if the floor were on fire, he slipped into the tunnel crawling as fast as a rabbit holding an egg could go.

Peter kept crawling until, at last, trembling and exhausted, he reached the other side of the fence. But he had his egg! Peter hid his prize under the branches of an old bush and, tired but happy, he limped home.

THE next day, Peter picked black-berries and squeezed their juice into a nut cup. Singing as he worked, he painted his mother's egg. Then he made a little basket of ferns and marched home to deliver it.

Mrs. Rabbit was surprised, as Peter knew she would be. "How lovely," she said happily. Just then, they heard a tiny cracking noise. As they watched the egg in amazement, a baby chick chipped a hole through the painted shell! "My, my, Peter," Mrs. Rabbit said, "this is even a bigger surprise than I thought." Peter just smiled, but he was thinking that his mother wasn't the *only* one who was surprised!

The Tale of
PETER'S SWIMMING LESSON

IT was a very hot spring day, unusually hot for that time of year; and Peter Rabbit just couldn't wait to go swimming. Even though his mother had told him, "No swimming until June," he just couldn't resist. Peter's ears were twitching with excitement as he scurried to the pond where he and his sisters always swam.

On the banks of the pond, soft new grass was springing up. Peter thrust a big rabbit toe into the water. It was wonderfully cold. He felt a kind of thrilling chilling.

PETER was enjoying this icy moment when a deep, hoarse voice startled him. "Watch out for the baby frogs!" croaked Mrs. Frog. "I don't see any baby frogs," Peter answered impolitely, for he felt that she had been spying on him. "They're just tadpoles now," replied Mrs. Frog. "Be careful." But Peter splashed his whole foot into the water anyway, and the ripples and waves sent the little tadpoles tumbling every which way. Then he jumped in, practically on top of them. "I can swim here, too," he shouted. "A big fat frog should stay on a log," he sang out impertinently.

PETER had barely turned his head around in the water when he crashed—wham!—into a line of baby ducks following their mother on their first swimming lesson. One duckling did a somersault, came up all wet and woebegone, and paddled his little webbed feet in a panic. "Baby ducks have no luck!" laughed Peter Rabbit.

MRS. Duck fixed her eye on Peter, spread her wings like great crooked hooks, and started after him. She hissed fiercely, stretched out her neck, and nipped Peter's ear! "Ouch! Ouch!" cried Peter, swimming as fast as he could to get away. Peter was a little frightened, but when he swam out of Mrs. Duck's reach, he called after her brashly, "It's my pond, too!"

"AND mine as well," an irritated voice snapped. "You are ruining my fishing!" Mrs. Cat was sitting on the far bank with a fishing rod, trying to catch minnows for her kittens. The little kittens were rolling and frolicking in the weeds on their very first day at the edge of the pond. "Move away," Mrs. Cat insisted. But Peter Rabbit paid no attention. "A cat eats fish, what a smelly dish!" he sang as he dove into her fishing waters and the minnows streamed away to quieter shores.

QUITE happy with himself, Peter rolled over on his back and closed his eyes to enjoy the sun. Suddenly, he heard a swish and felt something scoop him right out of the water. He was upside down in a fishing net! Mrs. Cat made a swift move and tossed Peter onto the ground, turning the net over on top of him. He was trapped. "Please! Let me out," he cried. But Mrs. Cat just smiled smugly and placed a big stone across the pole of the net, leaving poor Peter imprisoned underneath it.

PETER yelled and yelled. "I'm sorry," he pleaded, but no one came. Peter sobbed pitifully. Finally, he heard someone coming. "Help me!" he shouted. Out from the wood came his mother, Mrs. Rabbit. "Peter!" she said, "Whatever happened to you?" "Mrs. Cat scooped me up and left me here," he sniffed, not exactly telling the whole story. But Mrs. Rabbit knew what a naughty bunny Peter could be. And along the way to the pond, she had met the other mothers. "I think you're ready to go home now," she said, lifting the stone and flipping over the fishing net. Peter agreed.

WHEN he arrived home, pathetic and bedraggled, Peter didn't want to talk to anyone. But his Aunt Flossie was visiting with her seven little bunnies and they all crowded around him. Peter saw his little bunny cousins, and he remembered the tadpoles tumbling and the ducklings splashing. Just then, Mrs. Rabbit spoke to him in a stern voice:

"We were all going out to dinner tonight," she said, "but now I think you should stay at home and take care of your seven little cousins. I'm sure you agree that baby rabbits are very precious, indeed."